ROYAL

Bully

A MAFIA ROYALS ROMANCE
PREQUEL

by
RACHEL VAN DYKEN

Royal Bully
A Mafia Royals Romance Prequel
by Rachel Van Dyken

ROYAL BULLY
Copyright © 2020 RACHEL VAN DYKEN
ISBN: 9798632534413
Cover Design by Jena Brignola
Editing by Jill Sava
Formatting by Jill Sava, Love Affair With Fiction

DEDICATION

To all the mafia lovers out there,
this one is for you.

AUTHOR
Note

Dear Reader,

I'm obsessed, like losing my mind obsessed over my brand-new mafia series — Mafia Royals. I started writing mafia in 2010, released my first mafia book in 2011 on a whim, not realizing I would become addicted to it and unable to leave the world I created. It's been almost 7 years since I've launched a new mafia series — well guess what is here?

This is my very first standalone series that isn't owned by a publisher that I've released in years, and my hope is to introduce readers to one of my favorite genres, which is mafia romance. This new series is not part of Eagle Elite. Yes, it has familiar characters, and yes, fans of EE are going to be like holy 😳💀🔥, but this series is its own series.

I have four novels and this prequel novella planned.

Think mafia, bully romance, suspense, all in one!

Gahhh! Enjoy!

HUGS

rvd

WHO'S WHO IN THE
Cosa Nostra

*N*ixon and Trace Abandonato. Nixon is the boss of the Abandonato family he's a bit psycho, has a lip ring, and in his mid-forties, looks like a freaking badass. Think if Jason Momoa and Channing Tatum had a baby. SURPRISE, Nixon! Trace is the love of his life. Nixon's daughter, Serena, is his pride and joy, she's the heir to his throne. His adopted son Dom is ten years older than Serena. At twenty-nine, he's ready to step in if he needs to, but he really doesn't want to, not that he's thinking about a family of his own. His youngest, Bella, was a most welcome surprise.

Phoenix and Bee Nicolasi (formerly De Lange) have one son, Junior, and he's everything. The same age as Serena, he only ever has one thing on his mind. Her. But pursuing her is like signing his own death sentence. The one rule that the bosses gave all the cousins, all the kids, no dating each other, it complicates things. They all took a blood oath. But he's willing to risk it all, for just one taste.

Which brings us to Chase and Luciana Abandonato, their love story is one for the ages. He had Violet first, gorgeous, Violet Emiliana Abandonato. And then he had twins, God help him. Asher (Marco) and Izzy. All are attending Eagle Elite University. Violet is more into books than people. And the twins, well they are polar opposites. While Izzy is quiet and reserved, taking after her uncle Sergio in the tech support part of the mafia, Asher was an assassin at age twelve. He takes care of everyone even though he's younger than Serena and Junior. He feels it's his job to make sure everyone is safe, including his girlfriend, Claire. She's his soulmate, and he'll do anything for her. And don't forget the baby of the family, Ariel, who everyone dotes on.

Tex and Mo Campisi. He's the godfather of this joint, gorgeous, he's a gentle giant unless he' s pissed and his wife, Mo, is just as violent as he is. They have two sons, Breaker and King. Breaker just started his freshman year at Eagle Elite and he can't wait to release his own flirtations onto the campus. He's a force to be reckoned with, just walks around with chicks and shrugs. King on the other hand is vying for top whore at his own high school, I mean they say high school is supposed to be memorable right? He just can't remember any of the girls' names, so he calls them all Sarah. It's a thing.

Sergio and Valentina are also Abandonatos. While Val is quiet and reserved, Sergio is the resident doctor of the Families. He's also really into tech and loves spying on people. They have two gorgeous daughters. Kartini has her daddy wrapped around her little finger. He just hopes he survives her last two years of high school without shooting one of her boyfriends.

With Lydia, he knows she can take care of herself. She already beat up the class bully, making Sergio quite proud.

Dante and El don't have things easier, they're one of the younger mafia families, he's the head of the Alfero family. And he has two twin girls at age nine who are making him pull his hair out. Raven and Tempest are adorable, but they're feisty like their mom. He lets them have more screen time than he should, but they say he's their favorite in the world, sooooo... he lets it pass.

Andrei and Alice have been through a lot. Their name single-handedly brought the Russian Mafia into the Italian fold. Andrei is both Petrov and Sinacore, meaning that the oldest Italian mafia family is now part of the Cosa Nostra. Forever. Their son's name is Maksim, and weirdly enough he's a total flirt, he takes nothing seriously, but can flip a switch in a minute if someone he loves is threatened. Anya is his little sister, and he would do anything for her, she seems fragile but studies Krav Maga, so nobody messes with her.

These are the Families of the Cosa Nostra.

Welcome to the Family.

Blood in. No out.

CHAPTER
One

Claire

I was hiding behind a potted plant, next to a beer keg, and a
drunk frat brother who looked about one second away from
needing an ambulance. I drank out of the red solo cup—liquid
courage even though I wasn't much of a drinker, while I watched
him.

It's not like I was the only one.

Everyone watched him.

We may as well be servants in his Kingdom, and he knew it.

Asher Abandonato.

It had been years since any of the Families had sent one of
their own to school—one of the last guys—Dante, had left a blood
bath in his wake. Rumors fed the gossip circles until it was decided
that Dante basically chopped off fingers, thumbs, toes, laughing
all the while he did it, and then destroying everything in his wake

and don't even get me started on Dom, he was the last, some may even say the worst.

And ever since then, nobody was allowed to party at The Spot, or Space or whatever they were calling it this year.

Mainly because even bleach couldn't get out the bloodstains, and because others viewed it as some sort of Holy Ground.

Murals were painted inside the once famed party spot, just another way to cover up blood.

What kind of massacre took place at a University?

A better question? What kind of mafia family ran their own university and got away with it without having the FBI chase them down?

The Abandonatos were gods.

They owned everything.

Got away with everything.

And were too beautiful for words.

I bit down on my bottom lip as students watched in awe, Asher had taken one step inside the massive room at The Spot, and even the music was turned down like people were actually waiting for him to make some sort of speech. After all, he was a god among mortals. And we were partying in his domain, at his pleasure.

I sipped the tepid beer and watched.

They were waiting for something.

And I knew exactly what they were waiting for.

Because I'd asked him to come.

On a whim, during US History, when everyone was supposed to be watching the stupid movie, I'd dropped my pencil, he picked it up, our fingers brushed, and I jerked away in fear.

Fear that he was really as dangerous as everyone said he was.

And fear that I would have a violent reaction to his touch like everyone else did.

And I was right.

My reaction was completely uncalled for.

It was lust.

Not high school, oh goodie, I hope he kisses me lust.

But the kind that wraps itself around you so tight that it's hard to breathe, the kind that doesn't let up throughout the day, only increases with each breath and each step you take until you're sick with it.

Ocean blue eyes searched the room.

I stayed behind the plant, what the hell was a plant doing there anyway? They were partying in a room where souls were probably still floating around? The fact that the frat was even able to get in the door was astonishing; someone said they stole a key, and there they were.

The next day in class, Asher asked me for a piece of paper.

An hour later, he handed me a note.

"You're beautiful." Was what it said.

Who wrote notes in college?

He did.

Beautiful, dangerous, Asher.

With his wavy whiskey-colored hair and his massive build. He could have any girl he wanted, the guy could party with Victoria's Secret supermodels and fit right in.

So why me?

His eyes finally landed on the plant.

And then on me.

The crowd parted.

With a shaking hand, I lowered the cup.

And then he was there, in front of me, all six-foot-four of him, with muscles bulging in places that seemed impossible for a twenty-year-old.

"Hey," he rasped.

I had no thoughts beyond asking him what kind of cologne he wore and then dashing to the nearest store, buying it, and spraying my pillow with it like a freak.

"Hi." I found my voice.

Another step, until we were nearly chest to chest, I looked up into his blue eyes, waiting for something. We'd exchanged maybe two sentences in the last week. He'd called me beautiful, and I told him I'd be at the party tonight.

That was it.

"Dance with me." He held out his hand.

I stared at it. "You? Dance?"

"Don't you?" He grinned, his full smile was like a punch to the gut, no guy had a right to look so beautiful and lethal all at once. I could have sworn I heard a massive female sigh trickle around the room as I gave him my hand and walked with him toward the area where people were dancing.

He pulled me toward the corner, further away from the crowds, and then leaned in like he was going to kiss me. "You need to leave. Now."

"What?" I jerked back.

He pulled me closer, then twirled me until my back was to him, I could feel his arousal pressed against me. I froze as his lips touched the outside of my ear. "They're coming, and you're too pretty to kill."

"Kill?" I repeated.

"Stop repeating everything I say and listen very carefully." He gripped my hips with his hands and let out a groan. "Damn, I've been watching you for weeks." He bit out another curse and then seemed to refocus. "Nobody's supposed to be here, least of all a bunch of college kids degrading Holy Ground that my family is one hundred percent willing to kill over. Your choice is to stay in the line of fire… or leave… with me."

"And everyone else?" My heart slammed against my chest as drunken people stumbled around laughing.

"You care about them?" He seemed surprised.

"I care about human life, yes." This was happening, wasn't it? The rumors were true. Eagle Elite was mafia through and through, right along with a river of blood and tears.

"Interesting," he said before spinning me around again and pressing his lips to mine. I gasped as his tongue slid inside, mouth hot, I let out a moan as he wrapped an arm around me then pressed me against the wall, deepening the kiss, but also shielding me. He pulled away, his eyes dark. "My room's safe… you'll always be safe with me."

"Because of your family?" I was almost afraid to say the name out loud, not sure why, it was almost like I could feel the dead souls rise up from the grave, begging me not to curse them even in death. Blood had been spilled here.

"Because I have a gun…" He tilted his head. "Because of my cousin…" I knew who his cousin was, Nixon Abandonato.

And just like I'd conjured him, the door to The Spot jerked open wide, and there he stood, boss to one of the most notorious crime families in the world, and each of the four family bosses flanking on the right and the left.

Youngest mafia bosses in history.

They looked like they could still be attending classes, except for the massiveness of every single one of them.

"You have three seconds," Asher whispered, reaching behind his back.

"Yes," I said without thinking.

He grinned and then made a motion behind him, Nixon nodded just as the first gunshot rang out.

And then his mouth was on mine again, whispering against my tongue. "Close your eyes, princess..."

So, I did.

I closed my eyes as his hands slid up my shirt.

I squeezed them shut as the sound of gunfire went off.

I lost myself in his touch as he pressed my body against the cement wall, every inch of him hot and ready, his hands dipped into my hair, with a jerk he tugged my hair back his mouth made its way down my throat, and that's when I made my first mistake.

I opened my eyes.

And saw blood.

"Asher..." My voice sounded funny as blood stained the once freshly painted concrete.

"Holy Ground." Was all he said as he grabbed me and tossed me over his shoulder, walking through the blood, right past his cousin who seemed to look more amused than sinister.

Wait, were they laughing?

After killing at least a dozen people?

"They didn't kill anyone," Asher said, picking up his speed as he walked across campus, with me like a sack of potatoes over his shoulder. "All warning shots, more painful than anything, a few kneecaps blasted, a few arms hit clean through, nothing to be overly upset about."

"OVERLY UPSET?" I pounded my fists into his back. "What kind of psycho world do you guys come from?"

"Oh, that's easy." He set me on my feet and then flicked my chin with his thumb and winked. "The only world that matters—ours."

I gulped.

"So, what do I get for saving your life?" His full lips were swollen, I backed up just as he opened the door to one of the private dorms on campus, the ones that basically cost a billion dollars just to walk into.

I followed him.

In hindsight, a smarter girl would have run, but I was kind of out of choices at this point I'd already jumped in the minute he picked up my pencil… at least that's what it felt like.

But more than that, being with him was this heady experience that almost felt like a dream. With trembling legs, I followed him down the hallway.

And then his door was opening.

And I was walking in.

He clicked it shut.

I sucked in a breath when I heard the lock turn.

"Claire," he said my name like a prayer. "It's time to collect."

"I don't suppose you'd be okay with a high five and homemade cookies?"

His laugh was devastating; it wrapped around me, it pulsed like it was a living breathing thing. His laugh could knock every girl up within a two-mile radius.

I gulped when he turned me in his arms and tilted my chin toward him. "I like cookies…"

"Yeah?" That's what I had? Yeah?

"Mmm." He braced my waist, and then his hands lowered until he bunched my short jersey dress up to my bare hips and nude thong. "And I am hungry…"

"Do you have… chocolate chips?" I mentally slapped myself at his amused expression, and then he was tugging my thong all the way down to my sandaled heels.

"Fresh. Out." He grinned. "But I can guarantee this will taste better…"

"You sure about that?" I wanted him. I'd wanted him since he enrolled two months ago.

"Positive." He lowered to his knees, was this really happening? With a wicked grin, he pressed a heated kiss to my thigh, gripping my ass with his fingers, and then.

A loud beeping went off.

What the—?

I looked around his room.

And then something was hitting me with a pillow.

Wait what?

I jerked awake hot, bothered, angry, and staring right up into Asher's blue-eyed gaze, "You were screaming."

"Was not," I said a bit breathless.

He grinned down at me. "You often scream during a mid-afternoon nap, Claire?"

"Yes?"

"Ah, I see." He nodded. "I hope you don't mind that I let myself in, I heard someone say my name; actually, it was more of a god Asher, more Asher, I need you, Asher."

I felt my entire face erupt in flames.

I'd been obsessed with him for two months.

Two months.

But he was bad news.

Mafia.

On his way to a nice jail cell.

At least that's what my mom said.

I'd obviously glorified it more in my head if my dream was anything to go off of. Ugh.

"You sure it wasn't, go away, Asher?" I tried to appear unaffected.

And then he stood, walked over to my open door, shut it, and crooked his finger at me. "You look… hot."

"I'm fine," I said in a clipped tone as I tried to get the sheets away from my ankles.

With one swift movement, my duvet was on the floor along with my sheets, and he was hovering over me, his lips inches from mine. "Say it."

"Hmm?"

"Say you want me, say you've been staring at me for two months, say you've been dreaming about me." He slid his hand up my thigh, just like in my dream. "Say you're ready for me the way I am for you…"

I gulped as his fingers found my core. I let out a whimper, and then he really was kissing me while playing me like an instrument, in my bed, in my dorm.

"That's it, princess…" Everywhere he touched, I was hot, burning for him as he deepened the kiss, tasting like the perfect blend of bad boy. "I'm going to taste you like I've been dreaming of ever since sitting next to you in class—and I'm going to do it more than once."

I did what any normal girl would do.

I nodded my head dumbly and said. "Yes… please."

CHAPTER
Two

Asher

The first thing I noticed about her was her eyes.

They were brown.

Nothing really that unique about them, except, when they were trained on me, they widened like she was trying to drink me in and was upset at her body for failing her—her own eyes—for failing to grasp everything she saw.

I'd dealt with it my entire life.

The Abandonato Curse.

Being perfect on the outside and the devil itself on the inside—it was a problem unless you embraced the monster, then you were like a walking, talking, sociopath. Lucky us.

I nipped her lower lip, then tugged it with my teeth, liking the way she hissed out my name like a curse.

I could get used to her mouth.

I grinned, fisting her shirt in my right hand, ready to rip

it from her body and make her scream out like she'd been in her dream.

"Asher, what are you doing?" even as she asked it, she was leaning into me, her eyes dazed, wanting, needing.

"What do you think I'm doing?" I pulled her t-shirt over her head and pressed her back against the mattress, against the cool sheet, her dark hair looked like a waterfall of sin against the white pillow, her swollen lips were parted like she was waiting for more of me. "I'm going to take you."

"Take me, huh?" Amusement clouded her features. "Exactly where are you going to take me?"

"Heaven." I leaned down and worshipped her mouth. "Hell."

"Why both?"

"Why do you think?" I whispered in her ear as I trailed my fingertips down her exposed skin, unhooking her bra, then moving my hands to her jersey shorts. "Because you're…" She gulped her eyes locked onto mine. "Because."

"Are you really that petrified to say my name?"

"Maybe."

"If you can't embrace all of it…" I teased. "Should you really be tempting it?"

"I'm not tempting," she said quickly.

With one fluid movement, I had every inch of clothing off of her, dangling over the duvet with a prayer. "I think I'm going to have to disagree." My vision clouded as I tried to take her in, as I tried to memorize the glisten of her skin, the lust-filled gaze she gave without even realizing it. Everywhere I looked, more skin, the curve of a perfect hip, I breathed out a curse. "Tempting, so tempting."

She bit down on her bottom lip, sucking it between her

teeth and then she leaned up and grabbed me by the shirt, peeling it over my head, my necklace clanged against my chest.

She grabbed it. "Why are you wearing a horse necklace?"

"Because I'd rather not tattoo it on my ass," I said seriously. "We all have to have reminders of what went down, that night, the night at The Space." I didn't talk about it, not outside the family. None of us really did, it was on the faces of my uncles— on the face of my own father.

I liked to give him shit—but even I knew that could get my tongue cut out with a dull butter knife. Self-preservation and all that.

"You mean Dante?" She gulped. "The blood?"

"Blood." I laughed at that, as her palm pressed against my heart, and then I grabbed her hand and kissed the inside of her wrist. It was almost cute how little she knew; how little all of them knew. "I hope you don't have a weak stomach."

"What? Why?"

"Because—" I dropped her hand and hovered over her "— this isn't a one-time thing, so if you're out, I need to know you're out. If you want this, want me, then you don't get to close your eyes anymore, you get the ugly and the beautiful, they come hand in hand, princess. So—" I lowered myself over her, I gripped one of her thighs and spread it with my hand, then spoke against her mouth "—what will it be?"

Claire's eyes flashed before she wrapped her arms around my neck—I didn't realize I'd been holding in a breath until it escaped across her sensitive skin. A madness took over as our mouths met in a chaotic kiss that was almost painful. She pulled my hair as I kicked off my jeans, letting them join her clothes on the floor where they belonged.

And then, I was rolling her over me, letting those perfect thighs grip my body as she rolled her body against mine.

This.

This is what I'd been dreaming of for two solid months.

Every time I closed my eyes.

Every time I opened them in the morning.

Her.

On me.

Me.

On her.

In her.

Everywhere.

Only her.

"I wanted this." Her kiss lingered, why did kissing feel so much better when the person shares their words on your tongue? "So bad."

"Trust me, I know, you were screaming my name, chasing that ever-elusive orgasm the bed sheets and mattress really suck at giving you." I teased, and then we were kissing again, hands tangled in hair, bodies sliding against one another, I reached between our bodies as she gasped out my name again. She was hot. Wet for me in a way that made my body shake.

Touching her, exploring her, feeling her body clench around me had to be like finding heaven in a life full of torment and hell.

"Enough," I rolled her to her back, her throat worked as she reached for me, gripping me—hard. "Mmmm, keep doing that—" my hips moved "—I dare you."

She pulled her hand away, and then I was teasing her entrance, almost upset that this was going to be over soon, that this moment I'd built up—these minutes would tick by when

I wanted them to last forever. I was so damn hard; I couldn't think straight. Being inside her just may kill me.

"Asher," Her eyes glistened like she was about to cry. I slid into her to the hilt and covered her scream with my kiss. She was made for me, this girl, this beautiful girl with her pretty hair and innocent eyes. We moved in sync—chasing each other, clinging to one another for dear life.

I never knew I was capable of breaking.

Of letting go without keeping my guard up.

But she made me feel like I could.

And when she grinned up at me, teased me with her tongue and wrapped her ankles around me holding me tight, I knew I would do anything to feel this again—with her, only her. She was it for me.

A knock sounded on her door. I ignored it as her thighs clenched around me as her body sucked me dry, and she held on for dear life. I knew the exact moment she let go because I followed her off the cliff while claiming her at the same time.

Only to have the door jerk open. "Ah, prodigal son, good to see you're still getting straight A's in every sense of the word."

And I was still inside her.

Her face was completely pale, hey at least her bare ass wasn't in the air. It's the small things, am I right?

"Something you need?"

"Meh." He peered around me. "Nice to meet the girl he's been talking about since enrolling…"

I was going to kill him.

I flinched, reaching for the ever-present gun that wasn't actually present since I wasn't wearing any clothes.

I shot him a glare and flipped him off behind my back.

"Family dinner," he said with a gleam in his eyes. "Oh, and bring the girl…"

Hellllllllllllllll.

"We sure that's a good idea…" I grumbled under my breath, thinking of all the ways it could go wrong, number one being her running away screaming.

"I'm sure that's all that matters…" He flashed me an arrogant grin. "Seven, don't be late, I'm cooking."

My eyebrows shot up. "Ma's letting you back in the kitchen?"

His answer was to point to his gun. "See ya… son."

"Dad," I said through clenched teeth.

He shut the door.

Claire pulled a pillow and put it over her face. "Just finish me off."

"Suffocation." I pulled the pillow away. "Not glamorous, lots of leg twitches and panic, trust me, clean shots are the way to go."

"Who are you?" she said it more to herself than to me.

I just shrugged and got off of her. "Come on, you get to meet the Family."

"Dad?" She just had to say again.

"Right?" I smiled. "He looks like a brother."

"No, that's not…" She went completely pale. "Wasn't that…" She seemed hesitant to say the name out loud.

"Hmm?" I waited with amusement.

"Don't you think maybe you should lead with that next time? Hi, I'm Asher Abandonato, my dad's name is Chase Abandonato, make that scary as SHIT senator Abandonato, close to the president of the United States, and the only senator in US history to get away with murder and golf with the head of the FBI, yeah that would be good."

I shrugged. "He's just dad to me."

"How'd he find you?" She wondered out loud.

"Ah, they have eyes, ears, everywhere, spoiler alert, we probably have a sex tape now." I brushed a kiss across her forehead. "Welcome to the mafia."

"What the—"

"—clothing," I stood and started getting dressed. "We need to get ready; the uncles get super pissed when I 'm late."

"Uncles." Her voice croaked.

"Sure thing." I winked. "I mean, if you want to go naked, that's fine, but I may kill my cousin if he sees you naked."

"COUSIN?"

"Keep up." I tossed her the t-shirt I'd just pulled from her body and then walked over to her closet. "I'd go for something you can run in just in case."

Insert tense silence.

I glanced over my shoulder at her pale face. "I'm kidding."

She exhaled loudly then fell back against the mattress. "Not what I had in mind for a Saturday."

"We keep life interesting," I said, trying not to laugh at her scowl as she finally got up, moved around the room, and got ready.

I stared boldly when she changed.

The last thing I wanted was for her to put clothes on.

Then again, we were kind of out of options.

Within the hour, we were in my car driving toward the house. I figured we were hosting since Dad was cooking—it had always been this weird competition between my parents like Mafia Masterchef or something.

Claire was quiet next to me, and then she turned and blurted, "Are were seriously driving to your parents' house in a Maserati?"

"Don't hate on the car, she's new…"

"Ya think?" She spread her arms wide. "This is a dream, I'm going to pinch myself, no wait, a slap, I need someone to slap me."

"I don't hurt women." I shrugged. "So, unless you start slapping yourself…" I grinned. "What I wouldn't do to see you slap your own ass."

She shot me a glare.

"What?" I laughed, taking the next turn and hitting the accelerator. I was going forty over, didn't want to be late.

"There's a cop up—"

I laughed, cutting her off. "Who? George? Yeah, we're tight." I sent him a wave; he just shook his head as we sped past him.

Claire's jaw dropped. "What? Did your family pay him off?"

I snorted out a laugh. "Like we would even have to."

"I don't remember you being this arrogant in class."

"Because I'm bored as fuck in class." I pointed out. "Just like you are, it's why you purposefully dropped your pencil— have to say, not the most original, but at least it gave me something else to fixate on."

"What do you mean?"

"Your touch…" I shrugged like it wasn't a big deal when it was. And then she was reaching across the console and gripping my hand. I kissed the back of hers and let out a sigh just as I pulled up to the large gate.

I heard a holy shit out of her, and then the gate opened.

Ah, fortress, sweet fortress.

I pulled around the circular driveway and tried to imagine what she was thinking. The house was five stories, brick, a bit over the top with security cameras and men in suits scattered around the yard, but normal, completely normal.

For me.

I tossed my keys to one of the suits, didn't matter which one, they all worked for my family meaning they all worked for me—I was a little shit as a toddler, dropping my spoon, hanging upside down in trees making them chase me through the grocery store.

A real delight.

I opened Claire's door and held out my hand, she gripped it just as the front door burst open.

"YOU LYING SON OF A BITCH!" Tex, our Capo aka godfather, yelled as he laughed and made his way down the stairs, every inch of him was packed with muscle, the guy was lethal. Then again, all the bosses were. Tattoos and piercings hid behind expensive as hell suits and so much money it was almost exhausting to think about it.

"Swear jar." I laughed as I released her hand and went in for a kiss on his cheek, gripping his neck with my hand, forehead to forehead. "You know you're my favorite uncle, but I wasn't about to say shit."

"Yeah, yeah. And you told Nixon he was your favorite when you were five."

"Nixon bought me a real pony; you gave me a gun."

"I still think it was a better gift." He held up his hands and then peered around me. "So, you're her."

"I think?" Claire offered.

"Guess we'll see what you're made of, huh?" Tex winked, and then we were following him into my home.

It was loud.

Always loud.

So loud, a normal, sane human would need earplugs.

It was half Italian half wine induced.

And one whole bout of crazy as I walked her into the expansive gourmet kitchen where the uncles and wives and cousins all stood in astonishment.

Because I never brought anyone home.

Ever.

My cousins were my best friends.

My uncles came in a close second.

My aunts a close third.

My cousins and I were hell to put up with, and we knew it, so we stuck to ourselves, always.

Blood in no out.

"No. Way." My sister Violet ran full speed at me and then jumped into my arms. "YOU LIAR!!!"

"Love you too!" I kissed her cheek just as my younger cousin rounded the corner and grinned. "And this is why I win every family bet."

My dad slapped him on the back of the head.

Serena laughed behind her wine glass and winked at Claire while Nixon made his way toward us.

Claire sucked in a sharp breath.

Yeah, my uncles had that effect on everyone. Men were terrified, women were turned on, it was a problem.

He held out the blue bucket to me without looking away from her.

"No guns during dinner, not after last time," Nixon said with a smirk and flick of his lip ring.

"ONE TIME!" Serena, his daughter, yelled. "He stole the last piece of bread!"

I narrowed my eyes at her. "Do you think you need it?"

"That's it!" She charged toward me just as Junior, Phoenix's son intervened and held her back. "Let me at him."

Junior just rolled his eyes and gave me a, "please stop antagonizing her," look.

"Should we eat?" I asked the crowd, there were over thirty of us at this point, including the wives, the cousins, ugh, so many opinions and so many tempers.

Serena gave me the finger.

I blew her a kiss just as we sat down at the table.

I went to grab Claire's hand then realized she looked extremely overwhelmed, so I cleared my throat and said. "Roll call!"

Amidst groans and middle fingers, Serena and Dom both stood. "Those are Nixon and Trace's kids; Serena just turned twenty, he's twenty-nine and married, so don't even think about it." Dom winked in Claire's direction. "And the adorable eleven-year-old in the corner playing is their youngest, Bella. She was a surprise."

Nixon grunted, "Not to me."

Trace blushed.

"Ewww!" I plugged my ears. "Not at the table, guys!"

Nixon grabbed Trace's hand and kissed it. Never let it be said that the bosses didn't dote on their wives, it bordered on obsession.

I ignored them and kept with my introductions. "That's

Breaker and King, they belong to that dipshit over there." Tex waved. "And they both hate school."

"Hate," Breaker grumbled, his eyes flashed to Claire, and then he winked. "You know Campisi's got it better—"

A slap hit him in the back of the head from Mo, his mom. Damn, but she was violent when he flirted his way out of situations.

"Get there faster I'm starving to death," Maksim grumbled.

I sighed. "That's Maksim he's Andrei's eldest, he too hates school but skipped a year, so he's actually a Freshman, you just rarely see him because he's either in the library seducing upperclassman or reading. His two favorite subjects—sex and science, his sister is Anya, she's the gorgeous blonde sitting in the corner playing on her phone."

Anya looked up long enough to blow me a kiss. She was seriously going to ruin hearts when she got old enough to date, which was actually now, but Andrei kept her on a tight leash, he threatened her prom date with a tiger. A real fucking tiger. We never saw him again.

"You've already met Phoenix's oldest and only, Junior." I pointed to Junior, who lifted his wine glass and leaned back against his chair, all casual like he wasn't plotting world domination. "I'm sure you've seen him around campus."

Her sudden paleness said yes; she had, in fact, seen scary as shit Junior walking around campus.

"Sergio and Val's girls are the ones that keep fighting over the bread basket as per usual." I grinned. "Kartini's the oldest in her junior year of high school, and Lydia's a freshman in high school and has already been suspended for beating up the class bully."

Lydia and her dad shared a high five. Yeah, our family was weird, and getting weirder the more I introduced them.

Claire hadn't run yet, so I kept going. "And that brings us to Dante's two girls, the youngest of the brood, the most spoiled, and champions of Mario Kart two years running." I pointed to the nine-year-olds. "That's Raven and Tempest." I leaned in and whispered. "Their names fit, trust me."

"Heard that," Tempest said with a wide grin.

"And you already know my family." I shrugged. "Izzy's my twin, and Violet's a year older, she's at EE too, you just rarely see her because she finds books more fascinating than people. And my littlest and most spoiled sister Ariel is ten going on thirty."

"Ten, and yet, she can still kick your ass." Serena made a face.

I sighed. "I'm ignoring that comment since last time we sparred you limped for a week, by the way how are the freshman fifteen? Still holding on even though you're a Junior?"

Nixon let out a growl.

"Uncle Nixon," I held up my hands in mock surrender. "She kicked me in the balls!"

Serena shrugged. "You didn't like my shirt."

I threw my hands in the air. "I rest my case."

"So—" Phoenix Nicolasi, scary as shit boss interrupted with wine in hand "—Marco tells us you're from Seattle." Phoenix was the first to speak.

I let out a groan. "You did that on purpose."

He just grinned, like he liked throwing people under the bus.

"Marco?" Claire frowned. "Who's Marco?"

More cursing around the table.

And then a slap hit me in the back of the head, followed by another slap, a roll got chucked at my face—from my own mother before she gave my dad a look.

"Too Italian," I finally said.

"Damn it, Marco!" Nixon said with a grin.

"Fucking Marco," Tex added.

"Marco…" Izzy cupped her hand over her mouth.

"Polo." This from Violet.

I turned to Claire. "My full name's Marco Chase Asher Abandonato."

"I like Marco better," she said, probably earning the love and respect from every single family member at the table. Damn it.

I could have sworn I felt my mom sigh ten seats away.

"All right—" Tex stood "—let's pray and eat and drill her later; we've traumatized her enough."

I grunted. Ain't that the truth. I just introduced the girl I was falling for, to the Cosa Nostra. Most people couldn't even say they survived it.

I gripped Claire's hand.

She gripped mine back.

And look, I know we were praying and thanking God for letting us rule the crime world, blah, blah, blah, but I could still taste her on me.

Feel her slide against me.

I was at a family dinner, completely ready to swipe the food off the table and feast on her instead.

Maybe she felt my tension.

Her fingers inched across my thigh.

I jolted as her hand cupped me and then moved, just a bit,

the friction, her heat. I gritted my teeth. How long was this prayer gonna be?

"Amen," everyone said.

Her hand remained.

I narrowed my gaze at her, but she was staring innocently straight ahead.

Huh, two could play that game. And I remembered hearing of a few of my uncles nearly having sex during family dinners so...

I reached into her lap.

She jumped a foot.

"Everything okay?" My mom asked.

Claire's face flamed. "Yup, just... great... food."

"You haven't eaten anything yet." Mom pointed out.

"Right." She swallowed and shot me a glare. I shrugged and faced my uncles again. All the while pressing my palm against her in warning, I had no qualms about getting her off while thirty people wondered why she was having a heat stroke at the table, in fact. I looked forward to it.

CHAPTER
Three

Claire

The guy had a death wish.

Mouth dry I tried to look normal as I lifted my water glass to my lips, I nearly choked when he pressed down. The pressure was driving me insane, the need to ride his hand, move against him, strangle him…

And he seemed to love it.

The devastating grin on his face was almost too much to take in.

Did I put that grin there?

"So, how's Eagle Elite?" A guy that literally looked like he just stepped off a magazine cover high-fived Asher and asked, he looked younger than the rest of the uncles as Asher called him. I couldn't remember his name for the life of me. I just knew he had the youngest kids.

"Dante," Asher said under his breath with pride.

Ah, another scary one.

The one that took down several students on campus, who took over the Eagle Elite throne, then disappeared. The woman next to him smiled wide.

She was too pretty for words.

Who were these people?

What was this world? I mean, it's not like I wasn't accustomed to money, my uncle was loaded, but it's not like I lived in his mansion or on his yacht. My mom worked as a VP for his company, and my father was a surgeon. This was next level beauty, next level money, the kind that makes the world go round.

Or people disappear?

"Um, it's good…" I found my voice just as Asher pulled away his hand, Thank God. "We have US History together."

"Have you gotten to our chapter yet?" Dante asked with an innocent smirk.

I gawked.

"He's kidding." Asher laughed as chuckles erupted around the table, more wine was poured, more questions asked.

And I ate.

Or I tried to eat while all the powerful men and women around me asked questions.

More wine was brought an hour later.

A knife was thrown toward Tex's face, he moved out of the way then threw a fork back, nearly hitting a guy named Sergio who caught it without looking up.

"So," another one of the uncles, one who made me so uncomfortable that I almost hid behind Asher, spoke. "What are your intentions with Marco?"

Right. Marco. Not Asher to them.

"You do mean after I found them naked together, right?" Chase piped up.

Humiliation complete, I groaned into my hands; nobody seemed upset instead they seemed, excited? Could that be right? Parents who encourage wild, crazy sex with a relative stranger and pour their eighteen-year-olds wine?

"Dad…" Asher's tone shifted, it sliced through the room, the way he said Dad, his voice rasped, his tone dropped. And I realized, I was very much in over my head. These people were killers. This wasn't Marvel, more like Suicide Squad.

"I really like him." I interrupted the tense moment.

The guy across from me grinned. "Mmm." He reached down and pulled out a folder; it was black, and it had my name on it. "Understand that men like us are curious."

"Because I'm not Italian?" I wondered out loud.

The corners of his mouth lifted into a smile. "Nah, Claire, it's not because of who you aren't… it's because of who you are."

"Come again?" I wondered out loud.

"Step. Away." A familiar voice sounded. Meanwhile, I hadn't even heard the door close, what in the world? Slowly I turned.

A gun was held to Asher's head.

My uncle, on the other end of it.

I jumped to my feet, knocking my chair on its side.

His eyes raked over me, then he nodded to Nixon. "Thanks for the text."

"Figured the jet would get you here faster." Nixon just grinned like he was enjoying himself.

"Nikolai?" Asher craned his neck around.

"Uncle Nikolai?"

"Were you or were you not just having sex with my niece?" His finger pressed the trigger.

This was not happening.

Uncle Nikolai was stupid rich.

Famous.

Incredible.

My mom's boss.

I would do anything for him.

"Right, was getting to that part." The other guy smiled. "She's a Petrov… surprise!"

"It's like this family just can't stay away from Russia," Sergio said under his breath earning stares his way and a kiss from his wife.

"Um, can someone explain…" My voice trailed off when Asher winked at me and then gave Nikolai a playful shrug.

With a sigh, Nikolai lowered his gun and stared Asher down. "You're lucky you're one of my favorites."

Asher rolled his eyes. "We're all your favorite, you can't help it."

"Wine?" Nixon held up a bottle.

Nikolai took the entire thing, not taking my eyes off me. "Do your parents know?"

"What do you mean, do they know? It's been like four hours!"

"Five." Asher coughed. I glared at him; he just shrugged with a smile. "Sorry, I'm a numbers guy."

"Just don't ask him to go past ten," Violet said sweetly, earning an eye roll from him.

I was having a hard time wrapping my head around any of this.

My uncle.

Russian.

I mean, I knew that we had Russian blood in us, compliments of Nikolai and his wife, but still.

I frowned down at my hands. "Is this a problem?"

Nikolai burst out laughing while the rest of the guys at the table snickered.

"Yes, because Italians are a pain in the ass to deal with at Christmas, so loud… never any vodka."

"He lies," Sergio said in a bored voice. "We always have vodka; he's just pissed because it's Tito's…"

Nikolai made a face.

"What are you even doing here?" I blurted. "I haven't seen you since I left for school!"

He just grinned that good looking grin that got him on the front cover of People magazine and shrugged. "We all have our connections, don't we?"

Asher raised his hand. "Question, when were you guys going to tell me that her uncle has a scary amount of kills to his name? Anyone? Anyone at all?"

"Oh, that's why we called him." Chase flashed us both a grin. "You know, figured it was smart to have a legit doctor do the whole reasons why you don't have sex in your dorm room talk, then again I realized I didn't have a leg to stand on, neither does Nixon, Sergio, don't even get me started on cousin Vic…" A tall, brooding guy with enough guns strapped to his chest, rolled his eyes. Had he seriously been standing by the door the whole time? "And Tex well he just plowed right through—" A gun was pointed at Chase, "HEY! No weapons at the table!"

Tex shrugged, gun still pointed. "I'm the Godfather."

I mean, he wasn't wrong…

"Shoot him, Chase, I'm next in line." Another male voice snickered, earning my attention. Yup, all beautiful. Every last one of them.

"Dom doesn't have the balls," Tex said dryly.

"I don't need a sex talk." I felt the need to say. "Is this how every family dinner goes?"

Everyone fell silent as if the silence meant they agreed with each other.

I moved away from the table, needing some space away from the crazy, well that and my uncle's watchful eyes. Asher joined me, clutching my hand in his.

And then I found myself walking away while Nikolai chased Asher and me down.

"Hey." Nikolai grabbed my hand and spun me back around. "You know we're just giving you shit, right? I only flew down to scare him, and he's still wearing a smug expression handed down by his equally smug father."

"Standing, right here." Asher waved at us.

"You know—" Nikolai's face darkened "—once you're in… that's it, there is no escape…"

"Are you talking from experience?" I asked in a weak voice.

"We all have blood on our hands," he said somberly. "Some more than others."

"He's some," Asher piped up. "Just in case you were curious."

"Coming from the guy who had his first kill at twelve?" Nikolai made it seem like it wasn't a big deal. I dropped Asher's hand, my legs heavy, head swimming with questions.

Twelve?

Years?

Old?

I was still playing with Barbies! And he had a gun? Okay, maybe not Barbies, more like makeup, but the thought of it was outrageous!

"Thanks, Nik." Asher rubbed the back of his head with his hand and did a small circle like he wasn't sure whether to strangle something or just let what Nikolai had said take root in my mind. "Give us a minute?"

Nikolai bit back a curse and then turned on his heel and called back. "Get her pregnant I cut off two fingers and your pinky toe."

"Pinky?" I whispered hoarsely.

"Helps a person balance and all that." Asher waved me off like it was a joke when I knew that it wasn't—Nikolai meant every word, didn't he?

I frowned.

"Something wrong?" Asher cupped my face with his hands. "I mean other than the obvious." The corner of his mouth lifted in a beautiful smile, one that I wanted to focus on because if I could focus on that smile, then everything else didn't matter, right? It just faded into the background.

I exhaled a slow and steady breath. "Do you think my mom knows? About Nikolai?"

His eyes searched mine. "The truth?"

I nodded. "Always."

"I'm going to assume your mom and dad both know more than they're willing to admit. I'll let you in on a little secret."

I waited.

He licked his lips and lowered his mouth until I could feel his air, his words against my face. "Telling you anything about this life only puts you in danger. So, I'm going to bet they kept you in the dark on purpose. Not that it helped. They sure as hell aren't going to give you daughter of the year award for associating with me."

"Shoot, and I was so looking forward to the ceremony." I teased.

He captured my mouth like he couldn't help it then wrapped his muscular arms around my body. I sighed as his tongue dove deeper, his hands gripping my ass and jerking me against him.

Asher pulled away his eyes searched mine. "He always said it would be like this."

"He?"

Asher kissed my forehead and wrapped an arm around me, guiding me toward the back of the house, the suits as he called them ignored us completely, but each of them had earpieces in fit for the CIA.

"My dad." His voice was filled with pride. "He said that when you find that person, the one who reaches into your soul and refuses to let go—that you make sure never to give them any reason to run." His face darkened as he stopped walking. "His first wife…" He licked his lips. "It's why I wear the horse necklace."

"But you didn't know her." I fished. "Right? I mean that gorgeous woman sitting next to Chase is your mom?"

"Absolutely." He shrugged. "But it still bothers him, every year on that day, it bothers everyone that you could love someone so deeply so painfully, only to have them rat you out. Money…" He shook his head and looked down at the wet grass. "It wrecks the best of us."

"I'm sorry." I didn't know what else to say.

He was silent as we kept walking. I dumbly followed him,

at this point I'd probably follow him into a grave and go, cool we spooning while they pour dirt on us or what?

I was acting insane.

He made me insane.

I squeezed my eyes shut and let out a laugh. This was crazy. Wasn't it?

"How did he know?" I asked once we reached what looked like a pool house. Asher opened the door and then shut it behind us.

The thing was as big as my house back home. Two stories of perfection, flat screen tv, full kitchen, a balcony to kill for, and what looked like a sauna and steam room right next to a theater room.

Asher went to the freezer and pulled out a bottle of chilled vodka.

"He says she yelled at him a lot." He smirked as he pulled out two glasses and dumped a circular ice cube in each. When his eyes met mine, I almost backed away. He looked ready to attack, and I wasn't sure I was ready for more of him, because he was the type of guy that stole pieces of your heart before you consented to give them away.

It was terrifying.

Maybe more than the violence.

More than the look in his eyes.

The way he couldn't help but demand everything from me and expect me to just hand it over, all of it, his.

"So, yelling's the way to your heart?" I joked.

"You have seen my family, right?" He handed me a glass and let out an amused laugh. "To... new friendships."

"Is that what we are?" I tossed back the vodka like a pro and held out my glass. "Friends?"

Slowly he drained the vodka, his eyes never leaving mine. "Guess that's up to you... Nikolai warned you already, you're either in or you're out, no in-between for people like us, Claire."

"No pressure." I set my glass down on the table and then ran my hands down his shoulders, down his chest, feeling his hard-muscled stomach. Damn, the guy had more rivets than necessary, didn't he? Like his body couldn't help but build muscle on top of muscle even if all he drank was vodka and wine. In what world did an eighteen-year-old have a body like that?

He slapped my hands away and crossed his arms. "No playing without purchasing."

"What's your price?" I tilted my head, scrunched up my nose, and waited for him to say something ridiculous.

His expression sobered as his arms dropped to his sides. "You. I just want you."

"And then what?"

"And then we try to stay alive."

"You're serious?"

"Life, death, love, the only things you can count on... So... are you in?"

The question buzzed in my head.

And I knew it was one of those moments I would look back on and see myself standing in the middle of the road. One path led to a boring life married to an equally boring person, living in the suburbs and making pot roast. Maybe to some people that sounded great.

But to the left? I saw nothing but him.

Adventure.

Danger.

I could taste it in the air.

With a jerk, I wrapped my arms around his neck and pulled him in for a damning, beautiful kiss.

"Does that answer your question?" I rasped against his lips.

"You may have to do it again," He pulled his shirt over his head, then followed with mine, "And again," He was on his knees in front of me, tugging my skinny jeans down, gripping my thighs with both hands, sliding those rough hands down my skin. I had a moment of thanks that I'd shaved my legs the night before. A shiver wracked my body as his hands reached my ankles, my flip flops went flying, my jeans met a similar fate. And he stayed there just like that like he was seconds away from either worshipping me with his mouth or proposing.

I wasn't sure which was more terrifying.

Blue eyes flashed, Asher's smile was equal parts intense and sexy, I wasn't sure a girl could ever truly get used to being looked at that way. I couldn't stop shaking, and he'd already seen me naked.

He reached behind him and pulled out a small knife.

I didn't back up even though my heart told me to run.

He slid the knife across his palm and then held it out to me, still on his knees. Trembling, I held out my hand face up.

The cut was fast.

Painful.

The burn was almost erotic as he used that same knife, sliding it up my thigh until it came into contact with my thong. The sound of fabric cutting had me squeezing my eyes shut as the flimsy piece of material landed somewhere near my feet.

Blood dripped from his palm onto mine.

I shuddered as the pain dulled like a pulsing heat between us.

Drip.

Drip.

Drip.

With each drip onto my hand, I felt a high, like my body couldn't help but be tied to his in this supernatural and oddly holy way.

Slowly he stood to his feet, I swayed toward him as he pressed the knife between my breasts and with one jerk, my bra was cut in half. He moved the blade to the straps, I flinched with each tear.

And stared down at my discarded clothes.

The knife joined my clothes.

And then he pressed his palm to mine. I let out a cry of pain at his touch, the stinging was back, his mouth was hot and heavy on the back of my neck as he moved my hair to the side with his free hand.

Our fingers tangled as blood pulsed between our palms.

And then he flipped me around, his mouth hot on mine, his lips parted, tongue on tongue, fighting for dominance. He braced me against the kitchen wall, his bloody palm pressed against my heart as he lifted me with his free arm, I could feel his heartbeat through the wound.

"Look at me." He breathed. "Look at us."

I opened my eyes and stared between our bodies; a bloody handprint was pressed over my heart. "Blood in. No out," he whispered.

"Blood in." My voice shook. "No out." And then I unbuttoned his jeans sliding them down his legs with my foot.

"Clever."

"Just trying to be useful." I kissed him again, forgetting

that this wasn't just a one-night stand, sex, or even a two-night stand.

He was making me a promise.

And I was agreeing to it.

To everything.

No regrets.

"You're mine." He said through clenched teeth as he pressed punishing kiss after punishing kiss against my mouth.

I moved with him, gripping him in my hand. "Yours. Yes. Yes."

He gritted his teeth then thrust into me. No warning, no hesitation.

I sucked in a sharp breath as our bloody palms met and pressed into each other, as he anchored them against the wall along with my body. Moving inside me, claiming me in a way I would never come back from.

"It should always, always be like this." He vowed.

I let out a whimper.

"Don't hold back. Not from me." His lips were on my ear, then my neck, waves of pleasure pounded into me until all I saw were ocean blue eyes and full wicked lips.

Body shaking, I couldn't hold out any longer, maybe he could sense it, maybe he was just as close, with a growl he cried out my name.

My head fell back against the wall.

"Look," His voice was hoarse. "Look at us…"

I turned to where he was looking, and next to my head, were two bloody handprints in the shape of a heart.

"Blood in. No out." He whispered again. "Get ready for one hell of a ride, Claire."

"Didn't we just do that."

He barked out a laugh. "Yeah, I chose well."

"What? You were doing background checks for two months or something?"

He just shrugged, then said. "I'm his favorite nephew."

"What?"

"You really don't remember?"

He was still inside me, and we were having a perfectly normal conversation what was wrong with us?

"High School Graduation, I was in the third row, you wore pink. I asked Nikolai who you were, and he said over his dead body. I just assumed he was being an ass, had no idea it was actually because you were his niece. But he noticed... and yet here we are... nobody is sent to Eagle Elite by accident. They're chosen..." With that, he pulled away and held out his bloody hand. "Ready for an adventure?"

"Wait, you planned this?"

He pulled me against his chest. "Like I said, when you know, you know." He winked. "I just didn't want to pressure you into anything, and then I walked by your room and..."

I felt my face flush.

He grinned. "I'm an Abandonato. I get what I want."

"Arrogant."

"That too. Both start with A so..."

I smacked him on the chest. "This should be creepy."

He shrugged. "It's the mafia. We don't do creepy, we do scary as fuck, and for the record, I'm not letting you go."

"Do you see me running?"

He sighed; it was the first time I felt this guard slip. "No, but you should."

"How about we have more vodka..."

"Cheers to Russia." He grinned.

I smiled back and realized that this was where I belonged, where I would always belong, apparently—in my enemy's arms.

CHAPTER
Four

Asher

I chose my words carefully with Claire. I made her think it was more adventure less killing, but the truth was that we'd been in a war for years, one that none of us knew how to navigate.

And it wasn't one that made sense.

Because it was a war within our Family.

When the uncles started popping out kids, they suddenly realized they had the money and the power to send their kids anywhere, some of the kids studied abroad, some didn't come back, they didn't want anything to do with this life. And that was the problem, they were already a part of it, and we weren't allowed loose ends, and in the fucking end, we weren't really allowed a choice. Yes, you can study in Spain, but you sure as hell better come back here and join the fold. Because if you didn't, you were considered a loose end, and it didn't matter whose kid you were, a loose end was dangerous. Too dangerous to live.

I clung to Claire as she slept in my arms, and then kissed her forehead and slowly crawled out of bed. I made my way downstairs and wasn't at all surprised to see my dad sitting on the couch, knife in one hand, gun in the other.

With a sigh, I moved to stand in front of him. "Do I want to know?"

"I don't even want to know." He rasped, and then looked up at me. "I would have killed every fucking person in this godforsaken world to get you free of this life, but of course, I was cursed with a younger version of myself, wasn't I?"

I smirked. "Did you just call your favorite child a curse?"

He groaned. "Did you just call yourself favorite?"

"I won't tell the others." I uncrossed my arms and then moved to sit next to him on the couch. He had at least twenty pounds of muscle on me, and I was still a big guy, but my dad had learned a long time ago the only way for him to fight his demons was to literally beat the shit out of a punching bag and lift so many weights that he could compete and win against most guys his size. "Why are you really here?"

"I need my best," he said with a hint of sadness. "And the others don't have the stomach for it yet since you and I made a pact to protect them as much as possible."

I sighed as heaviness washed over me. "Junior already down there?"

"Yeah." He didn't look at me. "His intel's right, it's always right, the little shit lives and breathes for his intel."

"I'm not the only apple who fell directly off the tree into madness." I agreed. "Can Vic watch the house while I go in?"

"Already on it." My dad waved a hand behind him as Vic

made his way stealthily into the living room, gun raised. "Give us a few minutes, Vic, try not to scare the shit out of Claire if she wakes up."

Vic rolled his eyes. "I'll do my best."

"Well—" I held out my hand while my dad put the knife in my palm. "—let's get this over with."

My dad snorted. "Yeah, yeah, you have fun, remember, I didn't see anything... I'm clean now that I'm in politics."

Vic burst out laughing behind us.

It was rare to hear him laugh.

Then again, that was fucking hilarious.

I gave my dad a yeah right look and then grabbed the gun from him as well. "Go back to bed, hug Ma, you know I've got this."

My dad put his hand on my shoulder and then gripped it, pulling me in for a tight hug. "I'm proud of you."

My throat almost closed up. All I'd ever wanted was to be him, and all he'd ever wanted was for me to run away.

We don't always get what we want.

But I did, in this life, I did. Because when I looked in the mirror, I saw him, and I was proud to be his son.

"Thanks, Dad." I hugged him back. "I'll be quick, you know how it is when you have a naked woman waiting for—"

He slapped the back of my head.

I laughed and then winked at his amused expression.

With a sigh I walked around the house, the suits all gave me a wide berth, they knew what I looked like when I was given a job.

Complete focus.

Lethal.

I made it to the side of the house, typed in the code for the metal door, and waited for it to click open.

There were twenty-two stairs leading down to our dungeons.

Really, they were just bulletproof, soundproof, rooms with drains for all the rivers of blood. It was like a playroom for assassins.

My dad had taken me down there when I was eleven.

And at twelve, he gave me a choice.

Run or shoot.

I didn't run.

"Junior." I nodded to my cousin, who was flicking a knife with his fingertip and then Serena, who looked like she was just getting ready to sneak out to a club. "Serena."

"Stop looking at me like that, I'm wearing leather, hardly a crime." She snorted.

"You're two years older than me and look like a prostitute." I pointed out.

Junior gulped and averted his eyes. When I looked closely, I could see the smudge of lipstick on his neck.

Interesting.

Junior never looked unsettled. He and Serena were the oldest, which meant I looked to them for calm, and right now, they looked caught.

Ignoring it for now, I peeled off my t-shirt and handed it to her. "Even so, put this on before Uncle Nixon comes down here to murder Junior and me for having eyes, all right?"

"Gross." She shuddered like we both didn't give orgasms with one wink, and put on the t-shirt. Junior sighed like he was relieved, and I didn't miss the way his jaw tensed when his eyes flickered back to mine.

Well shit. Didn't see that coming.

We would have words about this later.

Because that was the one rule our uncles gave us growing up.

Fight, kill, bleed, destroy—but never, ever, look at any of the uncles' kids in any way other than like your own brother or sister.

The penalty was death.

And they were fucking serious.

I knew because I'd killed a cousin for it, at sixteen. He'd been obsessed with Violet, and she'd actually really liked him. Sergio found them together, and the rest was history. He'd been one of Axel's oldest. I was still traumatized over it. It's like his kids just didn't get why they had to become a part of this family.

"Let's go." I tossed the knife in the air and walked into the first room. He was tied to a chair. Axel Abandonato's youngest son.

He was eighteen.

He wanted to be a doctor.

But the Capo, Tex, needed him to at least be made before he was allowed to become a doctor, and if he did, he worked for the Family, for whenever we needed him, the point he had to be on our fucking payroll. Titan had been less than thrilled about that, then again, he still thought he had a choice when the only choice we had was in what way we served the Family. And running wasn't an option because running only meant they were giving you a head start before you got a bullet in your head.

"Hey, man." I walked in and clicked the door shut behind me, Serena and Junior watched from the monitor outside.

"Fuck. You." Titan spat onto the floor a mixture of blood and spit, he looked a lot like me, only he was younger and seriously drove me nuts, he didn't want this life, he wanted out.

Well, there was only one way out.

I stared him down. "This is what you want? Really?"

He glared. "Is there any other option?"

"Not really, no."

"Just make it look real," he grumbled. "And hopefully, I'll pass out sooner rather than later from blood loss."

I cursed. "Titan, you could just do a few jobs here and there, go to school, and then report back, it doesn't have to be all or nothing."

"I want to save lives, not take them." His stupid ass answer.

"Great, so now I get to rough up my own flesh and blood all because you think you're better than this?" I spread my arms wide. "None of us are better than this, this is your blood, Titan, your life. Once this is done, you're out of this Family, forever. You get that, right? And not because we shun you, but because you fucking die!"

I wasn't sure why I was trying to change his mind.

Maybe because he thought he'd be free.

Maybe because he believed the lie that we told the kids—that if they wanted out, all they had to do was deal with me. But he knew better. He was my friend. He fucking knew! I could see it in the way he refused to look at me. His eyes were glassy. He was done. And he'd decided.

Titan shrugged and looked forward. "I hate this family. The death. The blood. I want out."

Maybe I had an ounce of kindness left in me because I didn't shoot him in the head first. I shot him in both legs, then

I shoot into his right bicep, so his arm dangled at his side. He screamed out in pain.

And then I unleashed my knife stabbing him in the back over and over again, nothing deep, it would burn like hell, and it would triple his blood loss.

His head fell forward. "Still want out?"

"Go to hell!" he roared.

"See you there," I answered, emptying my gun into his chest.

I looked away as the last bit of life left his body.

And started to shake when Junior walked in and handed me the Bible. Serena's demeanor was calm as she recited our family Oath over him and blessed him as his soul left this earth.

"Blood in. No out." She whispered.

"Blood in." We repeated. "No out."

CHAPTER
Five

Claire

He was quiet, maybe he wasn't trying to wake me, or maybe he was just naturally that quiet, maybe he had to be because of who he was, what he did. I watched as he walked into the master bedroom and then moved into the bathroom. The door was open enough for me to see a reflection of him in the mirror.

I covered my mouth in horror as he turned on the water.

Blood was everywhere.

Splatters of it on his cheeks.

More down his arms.

He peeled his shirt from his body.

I sucked in a sharp breath, the guy had such a sexy body that it was distracting, which I needed, I needed a distraction.

Blood.

I almost gagged when he started washing his hands, staining the porcelain sink. Is this what I'd just agreed to?

He'd made it sound… adventurous, dangerous, but so normal.

But I hadn't seen death, had I?

Death to him was normal.

Washing blood off his hands was just another Tuesday.

My body started to shake as he continued to wash his hands. Maybe it was a nightmare. Maybe my mind was playing tricks on me?

I quietly got out of bed and moved toward the bathroom, leaning against the wall, so I could watch. Maybe if I just watched longer I would stop shaking, it would seem normal.

It looked like food coloring.

His blue eyes slowly lifted, locking with mine in the reflection of the mirror.

"I heard a noise," I whispered in a hoarse voice.

His eyes looked wild.

I'd never seen that look on another human before.

I started to back up as he slowly turned off the water and then turned, making his way for me. I made it maybe a foot, before his wet hands were on my shirt, touching my skin.

Trembling, I waited for him to say something else.

And then he cupped my chin with his right hand, I could smell blood on him, death lingered in the air. "Are you afraid?"

I gulped. "Yes."

"Don't be," he whispered. "It's just me."

"All the blood." I couldn't get the shaking out of my voice. His eyes didn't soften if anything, something else sparked in them, something… that felt evil and wrong so wrong.

"That's a natural occurrence when you shoot someone, Claire."

I gasped. "You shot someone?"

"It's my job," was what he said through clenched teeth, "I told you what this life was about, you swore your fealty to me, to the family, to this." He spread his arms wide. "And now you tell me you're scared? That you can't handle it? That you can't handle me?"

He was shaking.

Oh God, was this normal?

"Asher—" I reached for him "—what's wrong?"

"Bring me back," he rasped. "Please…" He tugged at his hair, his eyes looked crazed. "Bring me back, I can't feel—anything." His teeth started to chatter, and then he turned on his heel and ran his fist right into the wall, over and over again. I could hear bone breaking as blood splattered all over him, all over me.

Petrified, I reached for him, my mouth clanged against his and then we were a tangle of limbs as he held me with his good hand as blood dripped between our bodies. He pressed me against the damaged wall, pinning me there with his mouth with his massive body as it shook against mine. I coaxed him, kissed him softly. His breathing was erratic, his pulse the same. He deepened the kiss and then pulled back his eyes calmer, his focus centered on me. "I'm sorry."

"What's going on?"

"I need you." His voice was pleading. "So fucking much right now. I need you." He gritted his teeth and stared down at his bloody hand. "There isn't an escape. The more I do this, the more I lose myself. My soul isn't there anymore, it's barely existing. I don't know how to find myself anymore."

I held onto him for dear life, wondering what I got myself into.

Wondering how I was supposed to survive if he was already half dead, half gone.

"I killed my cousin." Asher's eyes saddened, "And I have a sick feeling, I'm going to have to do it again." He bit down on his lower lip.

"What do you mean?"

"We all have jobs." His voice was low, dangerous.

I was almost afraid to ask. "What's yours?"

"I'm the executioner."

Stunned, I just stared at him in complete horror and shock my mind reeling. "So, if I ran, after all of this?"

His nostrils flared. "Please don't do that to me, to us."

"Would you?" It was my turn to be hysterical. "Asher?"

"We all have jobs." He repeated. "You should go back to sleep."

"And dream of what? You chasing me down with a gun?"

"Please." He begged. "Not tonight. Just stay, let me hold you."

"You just admitted you would murder me!"

"Claire, you don't understand, if I didn't—someone else would. That's what I'm trying to tell you. There is no escape for us. And because I wanted you—I damned you too. What the fuck did I just do?" He tore at his hair again and then pulled away from me. "I'm going to go sleep on the couch."

"Asher wait—"

"—I do love you," he said in a sad voice. "But not enough to leave you alone… maybe I do take after my dad in more ways than one because he was never willing to sacrifice everything for the girl he fell for—and it seems… history has no choice but to fuck with us over and over again."

He slammed the door behind him, leaving me paralyzed in place.

Rooted to the floor while fresh tears streaked down my face.

What just happened?

CHAPTER
Six

Asher

I had to get myself under control, but I'd been out of control for a long time, hadn't I? I just refused to acknowledge how bad it had gotten, how I lost pieces of myself each and every time I saw someone's soul leave this earth.

But what other choice did I have?

It was the job nobody wanted.

Even Junior didn't want it, and the guy was even more bloodthirsty than his father, but that's another story altogether, isn't it? It seems that no matter how many of us kids try to break away from the sins of our parents...

We step right back into it.

Over and over again, like some sick cycle of torture.

I scared her.

And part of me needed her scared, I needed her to understand that the Family doesn't care if you're ninety or nine, they don't care if you're the favorite uncle, cousin, human.

Because when you know too much.

It's simple.

You know too much.

And we were done making an exception.

Because exceptions meant loose ends, exceptions meant emotions and feelings, and I knew that even though I loved Claire, even though I wanted to keep her, they wouldn't let me make an exception to the rules of this life.

She would be a loose end.

And she would die.

I just didn't know how to explain it to her without sounding like a monster. I could hear her tossing and turning in the bed upstairs. I forced myself to go to sleep and felt like I woke up ten minutes later when the sun made an appearance overhead.

I rubbed my eyes and sat up, making my way into the kitchen to make coffee.

I stopped when I saw my dad sitting at the breakfast bar already.

"It's starting to freak me out how often I'm seeing you these days," I grumbled, stealing his cup and sipping.

At least this time I didn't get a slap on the back of my head.

The sleeves to his crisp blue and white pinstripe shirt were rolled up past a maze of tattoos that made him stick out in Washington and well, everywhere.

"We're not in session." He sighed. "Got a few weeks left to tie some things up here."

I froze, stared him down over my mug. "What aren't you telling me?"

"What do you want to know?" His smile didn't reach his eyes. "She still upstairs?"

"Either that or she ran for the hills screaming, and I have

to go find her, yeah," I grumbled. "She saw me washing off blood, and I wasn't…" I squeezed my eyes shut. "The shaking won't stop. One moment I'm fine and then—"

"—you're human." He interrupted. "Never apologize for being human."

"It's not natural to kill someone you used to play tag with, Dad." Suddenly exhausted, I sat down next to him.

He wrapped an arm around me. He'd never been afraid to show physical affection to any of us kids, if anything, I got more hugs than I did slaps. Like he knew the burden he asked us to carry was the hardest thing he would ever do and that hopefully, by keeping that human connection, we wouldn't lose ourselves to the darkness.

"What are you really worried about?"

I gulped. "Her leaving. Having to—well, let's just start with her leaving. I mean we've known each other for two months; I knew it the minute I saw her, she was mine."

He listened intently. "And now?"

"And now I feel like I've fucking ruined her life."

"I could make it all go away." He sighed. "Sergio could help, but people would know. Andrei tries his best to keep a tight leash on everyone and everything, but we have people just waiting for us to crumble, to fall apart, people willing to do anything and use anyone in order to do it. She doesn't understand that our enemies would love nothing more than to hurt her. There is no normal, and since she's related…"

"Shit." I rubbed my face with my hands. "That's why you weren't pissed?"

"She's one of us. She has no choice son, had you not fallen ass first in love with her, we would have still had to bring her into the Family, you really think Nikolai would have let her stay unprotected that long? I know you hate school, but she's got Petrov blood, which means she will always be in danger from not just our enemies, but theirs as well. You know that the Russian dynasty is still pissed that Andrei, the last remaining heir, joined our side. His blood is both Italian and Russian. The fact that Claire's running around means she has a target on her back no matter what."

"Fucking Andrei," I growled. "He just had to go straight."

Dad smiled. "Say that to his face and get back to me."

"Hilarious, last time I teased him about shit, he broke my nose."

"He's young still." Dad shrugged.

"What does that make you? Ancient?"

"Careful, I could still kick your ass." He gleamed and then grabbed me by the neck and kissed my cheek. "Go explain to her, then get ready for school."

I groaned. "Still?"

"It's time," was all he said.

"Shit, are you serious? It's time?"

"The Elect." He gave me a somber look. "You always knew it would happen with you, with the five eldest kids, the five strongest kids. It's time to take your places."

"Hah, can I be the one to tell Serena?"

We'd been at Eagle Elite flying under the radar, but now he was asking us to rise up, to become the Elect, to run the school with brutality and ruthlessness. I knew what it looked like because not so long ago, my dad had done the same.

"She threw a fucking chair through the window, and Junior had to lock her in the bathroom to calm her down," Dad said with a wince bringing me back to the present.

My eyes searched his, did he know? Did he suspect? Last

night after everything had happened, I found them together, kissing, nearly naked, and I covered for them because I was petrified of what the bosses would do. "Dad…"

He looked away. "Leave it."

"But—"

"—I said, leave it. They're young, you're all young, just hope like hell it's sex and nothing more, because if Nixon ever finds out… if Phoenix—" He actually paled. "I wouldn't make you, you know? I'd do it myself if I had to, but I wouldn't make you do that to your best friends."

"It could start a war," I whispered.

"One we can't afford." He agreed. "Well, then, fix it." He slapped me on the back.

"You kidding me right now?" How the hell was I supposed to tell them not to keep having sex? Both Junior and Serena were older than me, and on top of that, the way he looked at her. It was otherworldly.

"Nah," He grinned. "Like I said, you're all young, emotions are hot, tempers are hotter, make it so they hate each other so much that they can't bear the sight of one another."

"And how do you suppose I do that?" My stomach sank.

"Make it look real," he said in a sad voice. "So real that she doesn't come back from it, that he's scarred for life." He looked up as Claire made her way down the stairs. "It can be your girlfriend's first job with you."

I flinched as my jaw clenched from grinding my teeth. "You want me to destroy them?"

"No, son, I want you to break their hearts."

When dad left, the small kitchen in the guest house fell quiet, Claire was making coffee. I went around her and hugged her from behind, my head rested on hers. "You okay?"

"It's a bit weird how often your dad stops by when sex is involved." She sighed, I loved seeing her in my giant white t-shirt, but what was better was the fact that she wasn't running away screaming... yet.

I grinned. "Yeah, well, he's just got really shit timing."

"You're telling me." She sighed, I could feel the tension in her entire body as she stood there, facing the backyard, our reflections in the window stared right back. She lifted her head and stared at me through the glass. "Tell me it's going to be okay."

"It's going to be okay," I said quickly. "And I'll do everything in my power to make it that way for both of us."

"I'm scared."

"Really? Because I wake up with sunshine sprouting from my ass—newsflash Claire, we are all fucking scared, and that's a good thing because when you lose your fear, you lose your humanity. Embrace that fear, it's what keeps us mortal."

"How'd you get so smart?"

"Hugs, not drugs?" I laughed.

She turned in my arms and pressed a kiss to my chin. "I'm going to go get a shower, wanna join me?"

I eyed her long, lean legs beneath my shirt and let out a groan. "I wish I could, but I have to go check on something, all right? I'll be like ten minutes; maybe if I run, I can wash your back."

"Is that code word for sex?"

"One hundred percent." I nodded.

She stood up on her tiptoes to kiss me again, this time on

the mouth, her coffee cup between us and I thought, damn, I would do anything to just have a simple life like this, without the blood, without the tears, without the fear that clung to us like a choking fog.

I kissed her back, promising myself I would do everything in my power to make this work, to keep that smile on her face, and then turned and made my way back into the main house.

Junior should be home.

As should Serena.

But it had been a super late night, so I figured they probably stayed the night as per usual, most of the time we crashed in the theater room, at least pre-Claire.

I didn't tell my dad that I knew things about Junior and Serena, that I suspected as much, that they had been dancing around each other for a long time and that I was the one that had to keep a secret about the way they looked at each other.

But this time, this time, I hoped they'd ended it, I hoped my dad was right, and hormones were just doing what hormones did. Fucking.

So when I quietly made my way into the main house and walked down the hall, I prayed I was wrong, when I slowly opened the door to the theater room and saw that the end credits to some horror movie were still rolling, I exhaled in relief.

That is until I heard moaning.

And saw a naked foot.

A leg.

And then I saw them.

Again.

Junior held Serena in his lap as she moved on top of him, her hair drawn to the side.

Shit.

My cousin was with Junior Nicolasi, and it wasn't a fling. A fling was one night, this was multiple nights.

"Love you," he whispered.

"You're everything." She panted back.

If I didn't do something asap.

Both of my best friends were going to get caught and die.

"As long as we both shall live." I heard Junior whisper gruffly.

Serena clung to him and repeated it back.

I almost hurled in the corner of the room, but made it back out into the hall and leaned against the closed door.

The dads would freak.

It wasn't allowed, but more than that, the Abandonato princess with the Nicolasi prince? It was a death sentence.

They didn't know what I did.

They didn't know the bad blood that was swept under the rug, perfumed, and ignored. Shit, they didn't know anything.

But this? This was the worst possible scenario. The main bosses would have overlooked a one-night stand, not this, shit, not this.

It was beyond infatuation, wasn't it?

It was real.

Which meant I had to make it appear real.

And I was going to break their hearts, break their love, so I wouldn't have to point a gun at both of them and say goodbye.

I'd rather them hate each other for the rest of their lives, hate me.

Then lose them.

My hands shook as I walked down the hall and back

outside to the pool house. The shower was still on when I reached the stairs.

And when I pulled back the glass door, dropped my clothes, and got in, Claire was there with a warm smile and open arms.

I could almost forget the death sentence on my best friends' heads if we didn't do this, so I kissed her hard, and then told her exactly what had to be done while she listened.

CHAPTER
Seven

Claire

"You want me to help you do what?" I asked with shaky hands as I zipped up my Eagle Elite skirt and grabbed my black blazer. It felt so foreign, wearing my uniform like everything was normal, like I couldn't still smell the blood on Asher. It had magically been dropped off at the house an hour ago, along with all the things I needed to get ready in the morning, like a creepy miracle. Huh, mafia.

I looked up, Asher was staring down at me with something in his eyes, I realized I'd seen ever since the first day we met.

Guilt and want, all tangled together in one tantalizing package that I'd taken, opened, consumed, and damned myself with.

"Claire." He ran a hand down my shoulder, and then pulled me into his embrace, lowering his dark head, he kissed me softly and then flicked his tongue with mine, I moaned in response, because even though there was blood on his hands, he still had the ability to make me want him, even though every single part of me knew that this man kissing me, would rather kill me than let anyone else do it.

Even though I knew that damning truth.

I still kissed him back.

I never understood the expression of a guy tasting like bad choices, like sin—but in that moment I felt it in my soul as his lips moved across mine, as his tongue massaged and sucked me deeper and deeper, there would be a point in my life where he would ask for more than I could give him.

And the thought was terrifying.

His eyes were dark when he pulled away; they stared right through me, so intense I wanted to shy away; instead, I met his gaze. "Claire, I'm not asking a lot, it will be easy, besides… the alternative isn't exactly my favorite option."

"The alternative meaning you get to go on a killing spree?" The words flew out of my mouth, he flinched as each seemed to launch themselves at his impenetrable armor. "I'm sorry."

"Don't be." He licked his lips like he could still taste me there, like he was making a point of it. "Especially when it's true."

I sucked in a sharp breath. "School's not going to be the same, is it?"

His eyes flashed, and then he was looking away. "No."

That was all I got.

Minutes later, fifteen to be exact, I understood exactly what he was saying.

We had pulled up to Eagle Elite University, and everything had changed, even the way the air felt against my face.

Serena went first; her thigh-high black boots were so tall

that I had a hard time thinking about walking in them, she stood in front of the black Maserati and crossed her arms.

Serena wore a leather jacket over her white shirt, her skirt was indecently short, and her cleavage was ready to pop out. Red leather gloves were tight around her hands, sunglasses were perched perfectly on her nose. Her black lipstick against her perfectly white straight teeth looked so intimidating that even though she'd always been nice to me, I was suddenly petrified.

Next was Junior, flanked to her right, arms crossed, looking too bulky, a bit broken, he stood to her right like he was ready to protect her, he locked eyes on her like he would do anything for her. He was all muscle, and for the first time since enrolling, I noticed an Eagle tattoo down the left side of his neck by his ear, his hair was buzzed short to the sides of his head, but on top it was long, luscious like a freaking supermodel's golden halo. And like slow motion, Asher moved to the right and held out his hand to me.

Me.

Wait.

I looked at his hand.

Then I looked back up at the two of them. Serena nodded slowly while Junior looked away like he wanted nothing to do with it.

His hesitation seemed wrong.

Slow motion, it was all slow motion, just like drinking poison and knowing it's going to kill you as it slides quickly down your throat, your life flashes before your eyes, you tell yourself you'll fight, you'll scream. You tell yourself that you're different.

And then the poison hits.

And you realize, you're just like them.

I took Asher's hand, noticing the cuts on both of us that bonded us together right along with the sickness in my chest that said I couldn't survive without him.

And just like that, the rest of the cars pulled up.

And one by one, all of the cousins got out.

Serena and Junior in front. Maksim, Breaker, Izzy, Violet, and us in back.

All wearing black.

Maybe because this was like their funeral.

Maybe because it was everyone else's.

I swallowed the lump of fear in my throat as the most beautiful and lethal people in the known world walked right up behind us, fully armed, and looked down at their kingdom. Evil grins on their faces like they couldn't wait to bring on suffering and destruction.

And I had to wonder, is this what their parents had in mind when they had kids? To make carbon copies of themselves? Or to create better lives for them?

All I knew was that the devil descended on Eagle Elite that day.

And I held his hand.

"What happens next?" I asked in a hollow voice.

Serena was the first to answer, she turned to me, handed me a pair of Gucci sunglasses, and said. "Whatever the hell we want."

"Yours to command," Junior said with a smirk like he was going to bow to a queen, and maybe, he was.

"After you cousin." Asher put a hand on her shoulder.

And I watched the princess begin her reign of terror as she walked ahead of everyone down a line of gawking students to take her place in history.

CHAPTER *Eight*

Asher

I would take it to my grave—but I finally understood what it felt like, that raw power coursing through your veins with each pump feeding the addiction, the justification for more and more until you're sick with it.

Students watched us in awe as we made our way down the sidewalk. Professors paled, the braver students pulled out their cameras and started snapping pictures.

Serena kept her head held high, her smug smile in place, I knew the princess had finally found her throne, and she would bring death and destruction because she was good at it.

Because she was Nixon Abandonato's firstborn.

Because he'd trained her well.

Too well as far as I was concerned, at least I wasn't the unlucky son of a bitch that had to spar with her, no that honor went all the way to Junior.

I watched them closely. I knew what we had to do. One

day they'd realize I was saving their lives, protecting us from a war, keeping the families together.

"I don't know if I can do this," Claire said, squeezing my hand.

"Tough shit," Serena said in a cold voice. "You made your choice, you're one of us now." Her face softened a bit even though she continued walking. "You've always been. You're Nikolai's niece, the fact that you ever thought you could have a normal life is laughable." She gritted her teeth. "We're in this curse together."

Claire licked her lips "At least we have each other."

Junior glanced behind us as four of our cousins followed closely behind. "We just brought a fucking army; they don't stand a chance."

"They never did," I muttered as more students started gathering around us. I leaned down and whispered into Claire's ear, "Play along."

She frowned.

Not enough time to explain.

It was the perfect opportunity.

My brain worked in violent, manipulative ways, and I knew all of Serena's hot buttons, she hated losing control, and she was jealous as shit.

She gave Junior a black eye when she found out he had to go to a strip club to grab an informant.

I always wondered why she was so pissed over it, now at least I knew.

I mean, the guy was there five seconds.

Maybe six, and that's me being generous.

My father's words coursed through me.

Break their hearts.

The opposite of love is hate.

I let go of Claire's hand and stopped walking. "Now's good."

Serena stopped and slowly turned to look at me, her head tilted to the side. "What?"

"We can't just walk by and make them think it's a fashion show." I shrugged. "That girl, right there." I pointed to a gorgeous girl with bright blue eyes and red hair, she was staring at us like she needed to get laid by anyone offering, so much sexual repression, you could feel it coming off of her as she watched us.

"He's right." Claire piped up in a strong voice putting her hand on my shoulder. "You need to make a statement, show everyone that you have the power, the control, can do whatever the hell you want."

"Junior—" I pointed to the girl "—give that girl what she's been asking for ever since she saw us walking this way, she's practically begging to get screwed, and she can't keep her eyes off you, own her, control her, give it to her."

"She's pretty." This from Claire, I sighed in relief. It was working out even better.

"What the hell kind of statement does that make?" Serena stared me down, I knew she was trying to figure out my angle, but saying she cared meant exposing both her and Junior, it meant admitting what they were doing even though it was painfully clear.

The last thing she wanted was for him to touch anyone but her.

The first thing he needed to do was prove he hadn't been touching her, and the easiest way to do that? Have the cousins watch him seduce the shit out of this girl, choose her, and then have them report back to the bosses.

The story would be legendary.

How Junior gave zero fucks.

How Serena encouraged it despite her broken heart.

Junior's eyes flicked from Serena to me and back like he was waiting for her to say no, to claim him, to say something like I love you, this is stupid. I wondered if he realized that his hesitation would be his downfall if he didn't act. His hesitation in front of the bosses would have given him away. His gaze fell to Serena again—I watched him steel his heart as if he was wrapping armor around it to keep it safe, to keep them safe.

And I knew it wouldn't work.

And it would be my fault.

A small part of me hoped he wouldn't take the bait, then again it didn't matter, he knew who his heart belonged to, sadly Serena wouldn't care, she'd see it as putting the family first, as cheating, as not choosing her even if he'd chosen her every single day for the rest of her life.

And Junior? His weakness was that he wanted to make his dad proud, he wanted to be a legend, was already halfway there, so when I said jump, he knew he had no choice because, in the rankings of our family, I had been the only one willing to do the killing myself, the only one to go in first, which meant I was a made man already.

Junior, however, was not.

Not yet, at least.

"Whatever, it's not a big deal," he finally said, then turned around and plastered a smile on his face that I'm pretty sure even made half the female staff clench their thighs together.

He crooked his finger at the pretty girl and waited.

She frowned, pointed to herself, then slowly walked forward.

Junior towered over her, all muscle and sex.

Her lips parted as if she was expecting him to kiss her.

"You. I want you for the day, maybe the night."

Oh hell. I kept my face impassive.

Serena reached inside her leather jacket for her gun.

She didn't pull it out, but I knew her finger had already flipped off the safety.

"Ohhh." The girl's voice was shaky at best. "Um, okay—"

He devoured her words with the kind of kiss that changes a girl's world, the kind they compare every other kiss to, deep, hard, and then soft, he ran his hands down her arms and then fucking thrust his body against hers before pulling her shirt free. With a wicked grin, he pulled back and then leaned down and ran his hands up her thigh-high socks until he touched the bare skin of her thighs.

She held on to his head.

A female professor started walking toward us.

When she was within a foot, she crossed her arms. "Stop this right now!"

"Stop what?" Junior didn't even look at her, "This is a university, right? Why would you discourage students from learning? Just think of it as hands-on—" he grinned as one hand disappeared under her skirt, the girl let out a shriek and almost collapsed against him. Holy shit, he was definitely overselling as she trembled in his hands "—experience."

Claire sucked in a sharp breath next to me.

I wrapped an arm around her and lazily watched with everyone else. Show no emotion, play your games.

Win.

"That feels…" The girl shook her head.

"—that's it." Junior grinned. "Hands, fingers too," The professor gasped as Junior literally had a sexual experience in the middle of the lawn. "Human Anatomy at its finest." He winked at her, then said in a low voice, "You want next?"

"That's it!" she roared. "I'm calling the dean."

"You must be new." Serena's voice was brittle, shaky, she was pissed, livid, shit she was going to kill someone today.

"Does that matter?" the poor professor said in a stern voice.

"Oh, buttercup." Serena burst out laughing. "How adorable!" She started circling her while I watched, while I let them do what they were supposed to do, while I pulled the strings. "Listen carefully, we own this school. It was built for us. This is our world; you should say thank you!"

"For what?"

"Letting you live in it." Serena tilted her head and then reached up and kissed the teacher on both cheeks and whispered. "And then, for letting you live at all."

"How dare yo—"

That's when the superintendent came running. "Serena! Darling! I'm so sorry, I had no idea you would be here so soon this morning!" He gave the professor a stern look and started to sweat. "Is there anything you need to—"

"—Fire her," I said behind Serena. "She's disrespectful. Make sure she's blacklisted, no references. I'll have one of my guys follow her home, you know… to keep her safe." I flashed a smile.

The professor looked ready to puke as I snapped my fingers, and Maksim came running. He was Andrei's. Happy for the most part, but loved the smell of blood way too much.

"Go with her," I barked.

He nodded and grabbed her by the elbow and walked her away. His eyes gleaming the entire time.

"'Bout finished back there, Junior?" I flashed the superintendent a smile while Serena regained her composure, hurt flashed across her face though when she saw Junior stand, tug the girl's skirt a bit, and then kiss her again, leaving her stupid and swaying on her feet.

"Not sure," Junior said with a rasp. "This one tastes good; you know how I like the responsive ones."

"So have fun with her today and pick a new toy tomorrow," Serena said in a chilled voice.

"That what you want, Serena?" Junior's arrogance slipped as he glared at her. "A new girl for me every day? Like a sex holiday? Because if you're saying you don't want a part of this, tell me now."

Shit. He threw the gauntlet. It would be so easy for her to just roll her eyes and ignore his taunt. He was shaking, with rage, guilt, with love for a girl he needed to claim. I didn't realize how much Junior needed her until that moment.

Choose me.

Be with me.

Fuck the world.

She stiffened. "Why do you think I care?" Her smile was brittle. "How cute, you holding a candle still?"

"So, you don't care," His knuckles grazed the girl's hard nipples through her white shirt. "Pity."

"Junior…" She took a step forward. I could sense her cracking, wanting to tell him to stop, that it mattered. That they mattered.

"It could be fun for him." Claire laughed. "Right, Serena?

Spread your oats? See what you really like, I mean, isn't that what college is all about?"

Serena gave her an incredulous look and then looked ready to hang her head and burst into tears as she whispered, "Yeah, sounds like a blast."

"All you have to do is say no, Serena," Junior said with hatred dripping from every word he spoke into the universe. His eyes were bright, unfocused, like every second she didn't run toward him, a piece of his soul was lost, a piece of his heart crunched beneath her stilettos.

I knew he wanted her to claim him.

I knew she wouldn't.

It wasn't in us to give up.

We fought.

And at the end of the day, Serena Abandonato, my cousin, had to stay strong, had to set an example. Her hands were officially tied, he'd already broken her trust, and now she had to prove to him that it didn't matter, because if anyone thought it did, they would know our weakness.

Each other.

"No, she's right." Serena leveled him with another chilly stare as she jerked off her sunglasses and grit her teeth. "Sleep with whoever you want, just wear a condom, and try not to get too violent Junior, you know whose blood runs through your veins."

"Serena!" I yelled. "Too far."

The fact that she even referenced that he had De Lange blood was enough to start a war within the Families. We didn't talk about rats. We didn't claim them even if they were in our own family line.

"Not. Far. Enough." She said with tears in her eyes.

Junior shoved the girl away and charged toward Serena.

She pulled out a knife and held it to his neck at about the exact same time he had one pointed at her right eyeball, nearly touching her eyelashes.

"Say it again, and I'm stealing something pretty," he roared in front of her face.

"Not before I slit your voice box to keep you from torturing people with your moans every time you try to get a girl off." Her lower lip trembled.

"You're dead to me." You could hear the pain in his voice, the anger. She'd been his world.

He'd been hers.

"I hate you." She spat in his face and then turned on her high heels and kept walking, grabbing the superintendent by the tie so he'd follow her.

Junior grabbed the random girl's hand. "Shall we?"

Shit.

"What have we done?" Claire whispered under her breath.

"Saved their fucking lives," I said in a sad voice. "Now, let's go to US History."

CHAPTER
Nine

Claire

The rest of the day past in a blur; by the time we made it back to the house or the compound as I was starting to think of it, everyone was tense.

Nixon was standing at the door, arms crossed, Chase was right behind him. I gulped and tried to keep myself from freaking the hell out when I saw my uncle Nikolai between them, Tex towering over everyone, and then it just kept getting worse as the sea of mafia bosses parted.

Phoenix.

Dante.

Sergio.

I knew all of their names now.

Knew the danger and weight those names carried.

I was surrounded by death.

I was surrounded by men and women who dealt with it on a daily basis, some of them with smiles on their faces.

And they were all looking at us expectantly, at me expectantly, especially Chase, his blue eyes flashed to Asher then back to me.

I gripped his hand tighter.

Only to have him release it suddenly.

What was happening?

Junior and Serena walked in behind us.

I could feel their anger.

I didn't know what to do, I knew I helped create the tension, I knew I fed the hate.

"How'd it go?" Chase asked like he didn't know. He wasn't looking at Asher, he was looking at me.

"Great." I swallowed the dryness in my throat. "I think we scared everyone shitless."

His smile spread wide. "All of you come with us."

I looked at Asher. He gritted his teeth and then gave me a slow nod.

We followed the men, the bosses quietly through the house, around a long hallway, and down dark stairs into an even darker basement.

The only reason I wasn't freaking out was because I trusted Asher and Nikolai.

The stairs stopped once we reached a huge room that had a long table in the middle of it. Chase walked around it and slowly started lighting the candles.

And then Tex was handing me one to hold.

My hands shook as I held the white candle out in front of me, Serena, Junior, Violet, Izzy, Maksim, and Breaker did the same. Asher was last.

"Sangue in non Fuori," Phoenix said in a low voice. "Seguimi."

I had no clue what he was saying.

The rest of the group repeated what he said, I joined in with a shaky voice.

And then he approached Junior, they looked a lot alike, Junior obviously inherited his parents' good looks and enough muscle to look like a professional athlete. "No more lies."

Junior's eyes turned cold. "No more lies."

Nixon moved to stand in front of Serena, he drew a knife down the center of his palm, blood dripped in rapid succession onto the concrete floor, he held out his hand. "Until another man gives you his blood willingly—you are owned by this family, your body belongs to this family, your very soul. Do. You. Understand?"

It was a horrible feeling, watching the last part of light leave someone's eyes and darkness take its place. Serena nodded coolly and said. "I won't let you down, besides—" her voice lowered. "—there's nothing more important than the Family." She hesitated. "Nothing and No one."

I expected Junior to have some sort of outward expression, a flinch of pain, something, anything.

Instead, a cruel smile spread across his lips as he stared straight ahead as if she'd taken every last piece of his soul and turned him more monster than man.

A shiver ran down my spine.

Because no matter how intoxicating the bad may look, how addicting, the truth remains.

Evil is evil.

Bad is bad.

And I had a sick feeling I'd just helped unleash exactly that. I couldn't look away from the two people I'd helped destroy.

I did it knowingly.

Helped Asher take the last shreds of innocence away.

I did it because I loved him.

It was still wrong.

All of it.

And now I was trapped.

With a guy I loved and would destroy for.

And people who expected me to do it again and again until it became my default mode.

Could I really do this?

Nikolai faced me, and then slit his hand and pressed that same bloodied hand against my cheek.

He leaned in and kissed the skin that was stained red with his blood, I could smell it as it dripped off my cheek.

And then something cold was pressed into my hand. "Survive."

"What?"

He moved out of the way. "A final test."

"Test?" I repeated my brain numb as someone sat in the dark corner, a bag over the head. It was clearly a woman; she was in a professor's uniform.

My brain didn't have to do the calculations.

I knew exactly who it was.

The same professor who had defied them today.

Asher took a step toward me, but Chase stopped him.

"Italians are touchy," Nikolai explained. "And you come from a Russian bloodline. Trust is everything, so prove whose side you're on."

"I can't," I whispered, "kill a person."

"She's not a person," Nikolai fired back. "She lost the right to her humanity the day she tried to defy the Families. Besides, I wouldn't make you kill her; that's Asher's job." I suddenly felt sick to my stomach. "Your job, as part of his soul, is to stand by his side. And as a token of your loyalty, you shoot first."

The gun shook in my hand. "I don't—"

"—lie, and you'll be next." Nixon intervened. "You were taught to shoot, so shoot."

I wanted to say years ago.

I wanted to tell them it was different when it was clay pigeons.

I didn't.

I looked around the room.

Damned if I do, damned if I don't.

I lifted the gun and pulled the trigger aiming for the lower half of her body, hitting her in the right thigh.

She let out a scream. And I knew I would remember the noise forever.

Because it accompanied the way I felt all of the light leave my body.

An exchange took place that day.

My soul, hers.

For the living breathing monster that is, The Family.

"You can't go back," Asher whispered sadly.

"Why would I want to," I responded in a harsh voice, realizing that I wasn't the only one broken, still breaking, something shattered between us that day too.

I just wish I knew what it was.

I thought about it later that night when he held me in his arms, when he wiped away the tears I didn't realize I still had.

When he kissed me like he was afraid I would disappear.

And when he told me he'd die in order for me to live.

Something was gone.

Missing.

I scrambled for it, mentally searching my thoughts, my actions.

And in the morning, I came up empty.

And realized sadly that it wasn't missing.

It was still there.

It had just quieted.

Because it was broken.

Bloody and beaten, just like the professor.

Asher and I had done more than just break Junior and Serena's hearts.

Mine was included in that scenario.

And I wondered in that moment, if Asher knew it all along, but did it anyway out of selfishness. Out of the need to have someone to share this life with.

And for one second, I hated him.

And then he was kissing me again as he woke up from a dead sleep, his hands on my body, his lips flush against mine, his hands sliding down my hips tilting me toward him like he needed my body in order to survive.

And I released the hate.

And clung to his love instead with full knowledge that if anything ever happened to him.

I would die too.

There was no other option.

Blood in. No out.

"You okay?" he asked against my mouth, his hands already pulling my clothes from my body.

His kisses drugged my common sense.

They made me forget about the death.

But my hands, they were still stained red.

I shook in his arms. His blue eyes flashed as he pressed an open-mouthed kiss to my chest.

I didn't realize it until he left to report to his father an hour later.

But the minute I let him into my life, I welcomed death.

When he came back hours later, his sexy smirk didn't do the same things it had done to me before, it made me afraid, fearful for what our future would look like, would we have kids and treat them the same way? Would he always look at me with love in his eyes? Or would a lifetime stuck with me only breed hatred after he realized his mistake?

Because things aren't always what they seem, are they?

On the surface, I was Nikolai's niece.

But beneath it all, I knew the truth.

I wasn't for this world.

I was too human.

Too humane.

And I knew, in order to stay with him, to stay with them, I would have to do the unthinkable, and already, I was testing the word freedom on my lips and wondering if I was strong enough to embrace it even though it meant saying goodbye to Asher forever.

Maybe that was my weakness.

My own inability to walk away from him when I knew it was the smart move to make.

"I love you," Asher took a long stride toward me, and then I was in his arms, and my thoughts were forgotten, replaced by a need to drink him in, because at least in the arms of my monster—I was numb.

"I love you too," I repeated, and then I wondered if this was my life now, watching behind my back, waiting, wondering.

His love was worth it.

His heart was worth it.

But I had to ask myself.

At what cost.

I gripped Asher with both hands as our foreheads touched. "Promise me you'll always be there, no matter what."

He trembled beneath my touch. "My life for yours, Claire."

"My life, for yours," I repeated.

A chill ran down my spine as I wondered how long that life would even be.

"Live in the now." He brushed a kiss across my lips. "It's all we have."

"Okay." I hugged him tight. "Okay."

WANT MORE *Mafia Royals*?
CHECK OUT *Ruthless Princess*,
SERENA AND JUNIOR'S STORY!

ABOUT THE
Author

Rachel Van Dyken is the #1 New York Times Bestselling, Wall Street Journal, and USA Today bestselling author of over 80 books ranging from contemporary romance to paranormal. With over four million copies sold, she's been featured in Forbes, US Weekly, and USA Today. Her books have been translated in more than 15 countries. She was one of the first romance authors to have a Kindle in Motion book through Amazon publishing and continues to strive to be on the cutting edge of the reader experience. She keeps her home in the Pacific Northwest with her husband, adorable son, naked cat, and two dogs. For more information about her books and upcoming events, visit www.RachelVanDykenauthor.com.

ALSO BY
Rachel Van Dyken

Kathy Ireland & Rachel Van Dyken
Fashion Jungle

Eagle Elite
Elite (Nixon & Trace's story)
Elect (Nixon & Trace's story)
Entice (Chase & Mil's story)
Elicit (Tex & Mo's story)
Bang Bang (Axel & Amy's story)
Enforce (Elite + from the boys POV)
Ember (Phoenix & Bee's story)
Elude (Sergio & Andi's story)
Empire (Sergio & Val's story)
Enrage (Dante & El's story)
Eulogy (Chase & Luciana's story)
Exposed (Dom & Tanit's story)
Envy (Vic & Renee's story)

Elite Bratva Brotherhood
RIP (Nikolai & Maya's story)
Debase (Andrei & Alice's story)

Mafia Royals Romances
Royal Bully (Asher & Claire's story)
Ruthless Princess (Serena & Junior's story)
Scandalous Prince (TBA)
Destructive King (TBA)
Mafia King (TBA)
Fallen Dynasty (TBA)

Wingmen Inc.
The Matchmaker's Playbook (Ian & Blake's story)
The Matchmaker's Replacement (Lex & Gabi's story)

Bro Code
Co-Ed (Knox & Shawn's story)
Seducing Mrs. Robinson (Leo & Kora's story)
Avoiding Temptation (Slater & Tatum's story)
The Setup (Finn & Jillian's story)

Curious Liaisons
Cheater (Lucas & Avery's story)
Cheater's Regret (Thatch & Austin's story)

The Dark Ones Series
The Dark Ones (Ethan & Genesis's story)
Untouchable Darkness (Cassius & Stephanie's story)
Dark Surrender (Alex & Hope's story)
Darkest Temptation (Mason & Serenity's story)
Darkest Sinner (Timber & Kyra's story)

Covet
Stealing Her (Bridge & Isobel's story)
Finding Him (Julian & Keaton's story)

Ruin Series
Ruin (Wes Michels & Kiersten's story)
Toxic (Gabe Hyde & Saylor's story)
Fearless (Wes Michels & Kiersten's story)
Shame (Tristan & Lisa's story)

Seaside Series
Tear (Alec, Demetri & Natalee's story)
Pull (Demetri & Alyssa's story)
Shatter (Alec & Natalee's story)
Forever (Alex & Natalee's story)
Fall (Jamie Jaymeson & Pricilla's story)
Strung (Tear + from the boys POV)
Eternal (Demetri & Alyssa's story)

Seaside Pictures
Capture (Lincoln & Dani's story)
Keep (Zane & Fallon's story)
Steal (Will & Angelica's story)
All Stars Fall (Trevor & Penelope's story)
Abandon (Ty & Abigail's story)
Provoke (Braden & Piper's story)

The Consequence Series
The Consequence of Loving Colton (Colton & Milo's story)
The Consequence of Revenge (Max & Becca's story)
The Consequence of Seduction (Reid & Jordan's story)
The Consequence of Rejection (Jason & Maddy's story)

Cruel Summer Trilogy
Summer Heat (Marlon & Ray's story)
Summer Seduction (Marlon & Ray's story)
Summer Nights (Marlon & Ray's story)

Players Game
Fraternize (Miller, Grant and Emerson's story)
Infraction (Miller & Kinsey's story)
M.V.P. (Jax & Harley's story)

Red Card
Risky Play (Slade & Mackenzie's story)
Kickin' It (Matt & Parker's story)

Liars, Inc
Dirty Exes (Colin, Jessie & Blaire's story)
Dangerous Exes (Jessie & Isla's story)

The Bet Series
The Bet (Travis & Kacey's story)
The Wager (Jake & Char Lynn's story)
The Dare (Jace & Beth Lynn's story)

The Bachelors of Arizona
The Bachelor Auction (Brock & Jane's story)
The Playboy Bachelor (Bentley & Margot's story)
The Bachelor Contract (Brant & Nikki's story)

Waltzing With The Wallflower — written with Leah Sanders
Waltzing with the Wallflower (Ambrose & Cordelia)
Beguiling Bridget (Anthony & Bridget's story)
Taming Wilde (Colin & Gemma's story)

RACHEL VAN DYKEN
www.rachelvandykenauthor.com

CPSIA information can be obtained
at www.ICGtesting.com
Printed in the USA
LVHW012033271220
675128LV00007BA/1306